YOUNG GUINEVERE

A PICTURE YEARLING BOOK

YOUNG GUINEVERE

By ROBERT D. SAN SOUCI
Illustrated by JAMICHAEL HENTERLY

For my editor,
Diane Arico,
whose expert guidance
has brought many
a manuscript
safely through the woods.
—R.S.S.

For my father.
—J.H.

Published by
Bantam Doubleday Dell Books for Young Readers
a division of
Bantam Doubleday Dell Publishing Group, Inc.
1540 Broadway
New York, New York 10036

ISBN: 0-440-41291-9
Reprinted by arrangement with Doubleday Books for
Young Readers

Printed in the United States of America

November 1996
10 9 8 7 6 5 4 3 2 1

ABOUT THE BOOK

I've long been fascinated by the *Book of Kells* with its magical illuminations painted by artist-monks in the British Isles over a thousand years ago. As I work at my drawing board today using much the same tools, I try to keep in mind that I am continuing that ancient tradition of illuminating word with image. The resonances were particularly strong while illustrating *Young Guinevere*, with its origins in the same period and place as the *Kells* images. So I used *Kells* style decoration in the book and strove for historical accuracy in other details as well. Guinevere working at her embroidery instantly called to mind the famous Bayeux Tapestry of the eleventh century, a style I mimicked in spot illustrations. I was delighted that Bob San Souci emphasized mythic elements in the Guinevere stories; after all, they arose in a time when the line between myth and everyday experience was very fine, and that is a sense I strove to capture in my pictures.

Jamichael Henterly

The text of this book is set in 16-point ITC Golden Type, which is a revival of a typeface designed by William Morris. He took examples of this Roman type from the great Venetian printer of the fifteenth century, Nicolas Jenson. Morris named this type Golden Type because it was first used in his printing of *The Golden Legend* in 1892.
Typography by Lynn Braswell

This story of Guinevere's life as a child and young woman draws on a
variety of classic and contemporary sources. It also reflects the
author's reading of the "might-have-beens" between the
lines of legends, folktales, ballads, poems, and
works of literature and history that touch
—all too briefly—on Guinevere's
early life.

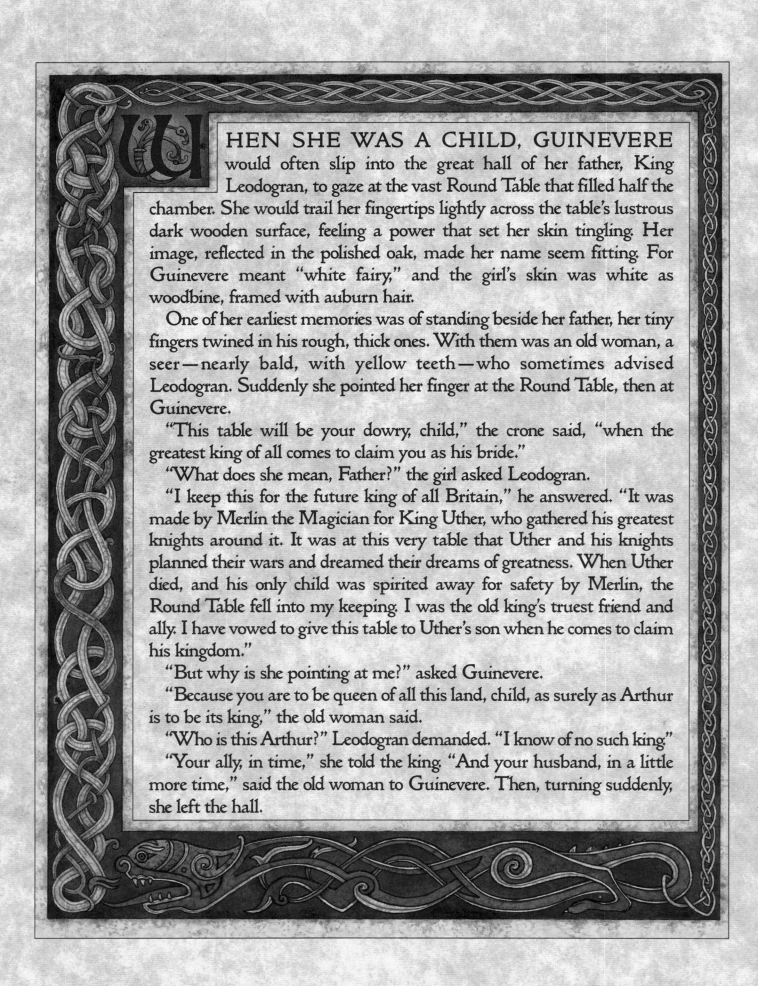

HEN SHE WAS A CHILD, GUINEVERE would often slip into the great hall of her father, King Leodogran, to gaze at the vast Round Table that filled half the chamber. She would trail her fingertips lightly across the table's lustrous dark wooden surface, feeling a power that set her skin tingling. Her image, reflected in the polished oak, made her name seem fitting. For Guinevere meant "white fairy," and the girl's skin was white as woodbine, framed with auburn hair.

One of her earliest memories was of standing beside her father, her tiny fingers twined in his rough, thick ones. With them was an old woman, a seer—nearly bald, with yellow teeth—who sometimes advised Leodogran. Suddenly she pointed her finger at the Round Table, then at Guinevere.

"This table will be your dowry, child," the crone said, "when the greatest king of all comes to claim you as his bride."

"What does she mean, Father?" the girl asked Leodogran.

"I keep this for the future king of all Britain," he answered. "It was made by Merlin the Magician for King Uther, who gathered his greatest knights around it. It was at this very table that Uther and his knights planned their wars and dreamed their dreams of greatness. When Uther died, and his only child was spirited away for safety by Merlin, the Round Table fell into my keeping. I was the old king's truest friend and ally. I have vowed to give this table to Uther's son when he comes to claim his kingdom."

"But why is she pointing at me?" asked Guinevere.

"Because you are to be queen of all this land, child, as surely as Arthur is to be its king," the old woman said.

"Who is this Arthur?" Leodogran demanded. "I know of no such king."

"Your ally, in time," she told the king. "And your husband, in a little more time," said the old woman to Guinevere. Then, turning suddenly, she left the hall.

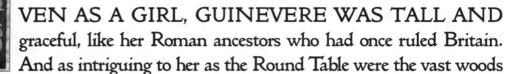VEN AS A GIRL, GUINEVERE WAS TALL AND graceful, like her Roman ancestors who had once ruled Britain. And as intriguing to her as the Round Table were the vast woods that guarded the western wall of Leodogran's castle, Cameliard. In summer, while she sat embroidering at her chamber window, Guinevere would note how the morning sunlight dusted the forest leaves with gold. And in the evening, a soft mist wound red-gold veils among the trees.

She listened eagerly to her elders when they told tales of strange creatures that prowled through the shadows of the woods. Or of secret glades where the fairy folk danced by moonlight.

On the wall across from where the girl sat at her needlework was a bow decorated with gold and a quiver filled with peacock-feathered arrows. These had belonged to her mother, dead seven years, and would be Guinevere's when she was older. In daydreams, she imagined herself a huntress in the forest — like the goddess Diana, whom her Roman ancestors had worshiped.

Because rumors of war worried Leodogran, he forbade his daughter to leave the safety of his castle. But courage, a strong will, and a certain impulsiveness were also part of Guinevere's inheritance from her mother. One morning, eager to visit the woods, she took the bow and arrows and slipped out a side gate, dressed as a serving-girl.

The sights and sounds and smells of the woods excited her. She tied her shift around her knees and bound her hair with a ribbon, like Diana the Huntress. Following narrow paths made by deer, she soon went farther than hunters and woodcutters dared.

By a stream, she glimpsed a unicorn; later, a magnificent white boar burst from the underbrush. Though her bow was at the ready, Guinevere knew such magical creatures must not be harmed.

When lengthening shadows warned of nightfall, Guinevere realized that she was lost. The birds' songs had died away and were replaced by the clamor of foxes and wolves. Fairy lights glimmered among the trees to lure wanderers into the snares of the magical forest.

Suddenly, rounding a curve in the path, the girl came face-to-face with a young gray wolf feasting on a plump bird. It seemed as surprised as she. It snarled at her and appeared ready to spring. But Guinevere loosed an arrow, wounding it in one leg. With a nearly human cry, the beast fled into the gathering dark.

Not knowing what other dangers might lie ahead, Guinevere drew a second arrow and then continued along the path. Soon she was startled to hear a child weeping. Peering into the brush, she saw a naked skinny boy, crusted with dirt. The child was sobbing and holding his leg, which had been pierced by an arrow. To her amazement, Guinevere saw that the arrow was her own. And she suddenly remembered stories of humans who could take on a wolf's form.

But there was nothing frightening about this hurting child, Guinevere decided. The boy seemed far more terrified of her, silently eyeing her like a deer run to earth by a hunter.

Softly and quietly, she approached the strange child as she might approach an injured hawk or dog. Then she stood still to let him take measure of her. Finally, she reached out a hand to stroke his hair. Thus she soothed him enough to remove the arrow and to bind his leg with a strip of cloth torn from her shift. When she was done, he suddenly bolted for the deep woods, as fast as his wounded leg would allow. "Stop!" Guinevere cried, but she dared not follow.

Soon after this, she saw torches and heard the shouts of men calling her name. A few moments later, she met one of the search parties her worried father had sent to find her.

Leodogran alternately hugged and scolded his only child. But neither pleas nor threats could compel his daughter to promise that she would never again go into the woods alone. Thereafter the king had her watched night and day, but Guinevere easily eluded her guardians.

And so she learned the forest's secrets. But even her courage and curiosity could not make her cross the Perilous River, which ran through the woods.

For on the opposite bank lived the Beast.

Some said the Beast had haunted the forest since the dawn of time. One old storyteller claimed he could recall when a careless magician, by casting the wrong spell, had created the monster. All agreed it was the strangest and most dangerous creature in the woods.

The thing had a serpent's head, a leopard's body, a lion's hindquarters, and a hare's feet. Once, when it came down to the river's edge to drink, the creature saw Guinevere and gave a cry like the barking of sixty hounds. The sound made the girl shiver, though the swift-flowing stream separating her from the Beast kept Guinevere safe.

On a chilly autumn evening, Guinevere returned to Cameliard and found the castle in an uproar. Horns sounded the call to arms. Soldiers milled around the courtyard. Servants ran everywhere carrying messages. The smithies, their powerful arms and leather aprons gleaming red in the glow of furnaces, forged fresh blades for spears and swords.

In the great hall, Guinevere found King Leodogran seated at the Round Table, deep in consultation with his knights.

"Father!" she cried. "Are we at war?"

"We are," he replied. "King Rion and his allies are at the gates of Cameliard. We are greatly outnumbered."

"Why is King Rion attacking us?" his daughter asked.

"Rion hopes to be ruler of all Britain. But I will not join him in his war against Arthur, who claims to be the rightful king, the son of Uther. I have heard that Arthur has pulled a magic sword from a stone as proof that he is the missing king."

Guinevere said, "Years ago, a wise woman told us a king named Arthur would one day be your ally and my—" She paused, blushing.

"Husband," her father finished. "But Arthur will find neither a friend nor a bride when Rion has reduced Cameliard to ashes."

"If you support King Arthur's claim," said Guinevere, "surely he will come to our aid?"

"By the time he learns what has happened, it will be too late," her father said. "I have already sent three messengers, and each has been slain by Rion's men. We are trapped by our enemies on one side and the forest on the other."

"Send a messenger through the woods," said Guinevere.

"None can survive its perils," Leodogran replied.

"Let me go!" cried Guinevere. "I know every forest path."

"Never!" said Leodogran. "To reach Arthur at distant Tintagel Castle,

you would have to cross the Perilous River, and that is where the Beast dwells. It would mean sure death."

"Rion's siege is an even surer death," said Guinevere quietly. "My way holds a slender hope."

They argued for a long time, but Guinevere prevailed.

Then King Leodogran had the wisest men and women called in, to tell Guinevere what they knew of the lands beyond the Perilous River and the Beast. They told her how to find the water bridge—a natural stone arch just below the surface of the river—that was the only way to cross. Beyond this, the king's advisors offered many warnings but little help.

Just before dawn the following day, father and daughter embraced one last time. Outside the walls, they could hear the clank of armor and groan of lumber as Rion's men built siege engines to breach Leodogran's defenses.

Guinevere rode her favorite black-gray steed into the chilly woods along paths of thick mud. Many of the trees had shed their leaves and were draped with chilly, sour mist. When low-hanging branches blocked the way, the young woman dismounted and led her horse on foot. Daybreak brought thunder and a light fall of rain.

At noon, she found the water bridge guarded by a gray wolf. But when she drew her bow, the wolf whined and lowered its muzzle to its paws, as if bowing to her. From the scar on one leg, she recognized the wolf-child whose life she had spared.

"Come with me," she invited. "I welcome your company."

And so, on foot, she guided horse and wolf across the Perilous River.

As she remounted, the Beast came raging out of the misty woods. Guinevere's horse reared, and she was hardly able to keep her seat. But the wolf bared its teeth and circled the monster, vexing it.

Though frightened, Guinevere imagined how her mother or Diana the Huntress would react. She forced herself to steady her hand and eye as she drew her bow.

Her first arrow went wide, as the Beast leapt. Its huge serpent jaws snapped at her horse's flank.

She fired another arrow, which grazed the creature's side, angering it. She shot a third time, but the Beast eluded her shaft. Then its jaws almost closed upon her, but the wolf bit the Beast's hind leg, distracting it. Guinevere thrust her bow into the creature's mouth, forcing its jaws apart.

In a fury, the monster clawed at the bow. Guinevere wheeled her horse around and galloped away along the river's edge, with the wolf following. She did not stop until she was sure the monster had given up the chase.

When they had rested, the wolf led her across a bleak landscape of lightning-blasted trees, where ghastly shapes loomed out of the twilight. But the wolf's ferocity drove them off.

At moonrise, she reached the edge of the forest, and heard the distant roar of the ocean. Here, she and the wolf-child parted company. She knelt and hugged her companion, whispering her thanks for his help. Then she galloped north along the sea cliffs toward distant Tintagel Castle, where King Arthur held court.

On the second day, weary and haggard, she reached Tintagel, where she was brought before King Arthur. His red-gold hair was bound by a circlet of gold. His honest face looked as rugged as the sea cliff on which the castle perched. But his blue eyes were warm and intelligent. As she explained why she had come, Guinevere found his gaze so intense that she grew uneasy, knowing she must look like a wild woman, with leaves tangled in her hair and mud daubing her cloak.

But Arthur said, with a grim smile, "Eleven kings challenged Rion's claim to be ruler of all Britain. He bested each, and now they fight beside him. But he will learn that I am more than a match for him."

Rising from his throne, Arthur shouted, "Tomorrow we ride for Cameliard, and fair Guinevere rides with us!"

When they reached Cameliard, they found the castle's defenders bravely resisting King Rion's forces. But Guinevere could see from the shattered battlements and the few soldiers upon them that the end was near.

While Arthur positioned his men, Guinevere circled around through the woods and returned to Leodogran by a secret passage.

From the highest tower, father and daughter watched as King Arthur's army—like a silver ocean with sunlight glinting off spears and shields and helmets—rushed toward the bristling shore of Rion's army.

Guinevere saw Arthur, in golden armor, and Merlin the Magician, in the shape of a terrifying giant, lead the battle against Rion's knights. The sky echoed with the blare of trumpets and clash of arms. The smoke and dust of battle turned the air black. The wounded and dying howled like a mountain wind.

The battle raged all day, until Rion's remaining troops and allies fled east and south and north.

In the evening, at her father's request, Guinevere carried a silver bowl of water and towels of green and white linen to Arthur's chamber. She offered to wash his face and neck. But the young king, in conversation with Merlin, politely refused. Only when Merlin insisted it was the custom did Arthur submit—clearly embarrassed—while the young woman washed away the battle grime.

Though they exchanged few words, Guinevere felt her heart go out to the king. She wished she could wash away the weariness and care in his face as easily as she could the dust. When she caught him staring at her, her hand began to shake.

"Let me go and get fresh water," she said, making an excuse to leave. Guinevere felt she could hardly breathe, she was so overcome with emotion.

Returning, she paused outside the partly open door when she heard Arthur say to Merlin, "I love the king's daughter, Guinevere. She is the fairest lady that ever I could find."

"Sire," said Merlin, "she is as bright as a blossom on a briar. And King Leodogran has guarded well the Round Table that I made for your father."

Behind the door, Guinevere blushed deeply. Merlin's next words, though, struck her to the heart.

"But I warn you not to take the girl to wife. You know well my power to gaze into the future and see what may or will come to pass. Guinevere, though she does not intend it, may be a greater danger to you and your kingdom than any rebel king."

"Why do you place such a burden on me?" Arthur demanded angrily.

"I merely place the facts before you," said Merlin. "You must be the one to choose."

"Though what you have foreseen may never come to pass," said the king, deeply troubled, "I dare not risk my kingdom."

Hearing this, Guinevere fled to her own chambers.

Because she could not disgrace her father by staying away from the feast in the great hall that night, Guinevere attended in her finest gown of yellow satin. She sat on the dais at her father's left hand, while Arthur sat at Leodogran's right.

Though she would not look at Arthur, she felt him watching her all during the banquet. And she was also aware of Merlin's gaze. She hardly tasted the fine food and drink, and made an excuse to retire early.

In the gray morning, King Arthur rode away with his knights, while Guinevere watched from her chamber window. Listlessly, she took up her neglected embroidery.

The first snows of winter fell soon after, but the ghostly woods in their mantles of white held no allure for the young woman, who plied her needle endlessly.

Leodogran tried to coax his daughter out on a winter hunt, but she had no heart for it. She sat in the frosty light, stitching fanciful pictures of knights and ladies, kings and queens.

She barely noticed when winter melted into spring. But one day in early May, she was distracted from her labors by the sound of festive horns. From her window, Guinevere saw a column of knights approaching. Their armor gleamed, while their bright plumes trailed in the breeze behind them. At the head of the column rode Merlin in robes of deepest blue.

Soon Leodogran sent for his daughter. In the great hall, he announced, "King Arthur has asked for your hand in marriage. And he has sent Merlin and fifty knights to escort you to the castle he is building, called 'Camelot.' I have already given my consent. But the final choice is yours. Will you go to Camelot to be wed?"

Then Merlin spoke: "King Arthur has commanded me to give you this." He held out to Guinevere a necklace of thick gold braid.

Her eyes met Merlin's in an unspoken question.

Merlin nodded, then said gently, "The king's heart is set, and he has made his choice."

"And if I say 'no'?" asked Guinevere.

"You will destroy him and his dreams," the magician said.

"Then, my answer is 'yes,'" she replied.

Three days later, Guinevere rode out from Cameliard on her black-gray steed, with Merlin by her side. Upon her head was a circlet of gold from Leodogran, and at her throat was the gold necklace from Arthur.

Under a canopy of silk, seated upon a jeweled saddle, she was gowned in green silk embroidered with gold. In addition to the fifty knights, Guinevere was escorted by forty maidens in rainbow silks adorned with silver flowers.

Because Leodogran had to remain and rebuild his war-shattered kingdom, father and daughter had parted tearfully.

"I am leaving so much here," said Guinevere.

But Leodogran only shook his head and said, "Your greatest moments are yet to come."

Now, behind her, Cameliard and the haunted woods dwindled and were lost to view. But the Maytime world ahead was green and white, brimming with blossoms and sunshine and promise.

AUTHOR'S NOTE

Much came to pass, as both Merlin and Leodogran had foreseen.
Guinevere became one of the greatest queens in legendry, and
she helped make King Arthur's court at Camelot the bright,
shining hope of a strife-torn nation. Yet she became—
through the impulsiveness of her own heart and the
plots of Arthur's enemies—the cause of the war
that destroyed Arthur's kingdom. Guinevere
spent her final years in prayer and silence in a
nunnery. The grievously wounded Arthur
was borne away to the fabled island of
Avalon after the last battle. From
thence, legend has it, he will
return to lead Britain in
her hour of greatest
need.